For Larry & Pops, an Unlimited Lifetime Guarantee
—with love always, Chan

For my dad (who also tells the same
old jokes over and over) —A.S.

A FEIWEL AND FRIENDS BOOK
An imprint of Macmillan Publishing Group, LLC

Our books may be purchased in bulk for promotional, educational, or business use. Please contact your local bookseller
or the Macmillan Corporate and Premium Sales Department at (800) 221-7945 ext. 5442 or by e-mail
at MacmillanSpecialMarkets@macmillan.com.

Library of Congress Cataloging-in-Publication Data is available.

ISBN 978-1-250-05889-8

Book design by Eileen Savage
Feiwel and Friends logo designed by Filomena Tuosto

First Edition—2017

The illustrations in this book were done in ink and digitally.

1 3 5 7 9 10 8 6 4 2

mackids.com

Daddy DEPOT

by CHANA STIEFEL

illustrated by ANDY SNAIR

Feiwel and Friends
New York

Lizzie loved her dad, but he was always watching football.

"Hey, Lizzie-poo. What's invisible and smells like bananas? A monkey burp! Ha-ha-ha!"

Whenever Dad made banana pancakes,
he served them with the same old joke.

"Ewww!"

"Lizzie-poo?"

At snuggle time, Lizzie told Dad about her moon project. But he just snored . . . *in her ear*!

Then Lizzie saw an ad:

····· Come to ·····
★ Daddy **DEPOT** ★
THE DAD MEGASTORE!

*From Acrobats to Zookeepers, we have the
perfect dad for you! Exchange your old
dad for a brand-new one . . . TODAY!*

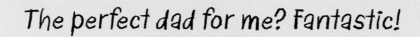

Lizzie put on her lucky tutu,

rolled Dad into her red wagon . . .

and pulled him all the way to Daddy Depot.

Daddy DEPOT

It. Was. Huge.

Lizzie parked Dad by the goofy tie display and took off on her shopping spree.

She heard an electric guitar playing in aisle 12.
She danced over and found . . .
Rocker Dad!

Lizzie tried to get close, but five bodyguards blocked her way.

Next Lizzie spotted a dad *floating* above aisle 43.
It was Astro Dad!

Wow! A dad who can blast off into outer space!

Excuse me, Astro Dad, could you bring me a moon rock?

"Sure! I'll be back in six months."

Six months? Still not the perfect dad for me.

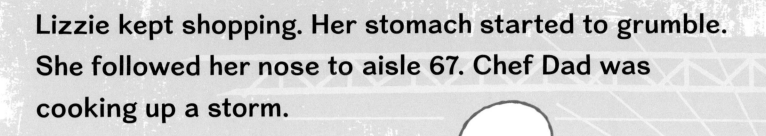

Lizzie kept shopping. Her stomach started to grumble. She followed her nose to aisle 67. Chef Dad was cooking up a storm.

"Try *zis!* Eet's *pâté pescerino bleu.*"

Delicious! What's in it?

"Mashed liver, sardines, and a shprinkle of moldy cheese."

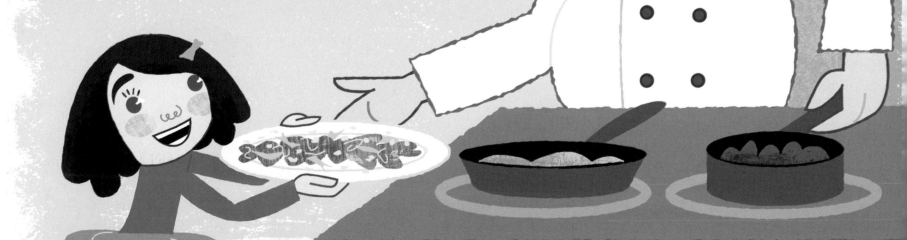

Lizzie's tummy was as empty as her cart.
Just then, a bow tie floated down to her feet.

Up, up, up Lizzie climbed to the top shelf.

It was a dad party!
There were all kinds of dads.

Lizzie searched the crowd
for the perfect dad.

She even twirled in her lucky tutu. But not a single dad noticed.

Except . . . one dad . . . over by the punch and chips . . . who was waving his arms and doing a funky-chicken-touchdown dance.

Lizzie's heart did a loop-de-loop. Only one dad in the entire universe danced like that.

Lizzie took a flying leap into her dad's open arms.

"Shall we dance, Lizzie-poo?"

YOU are the perfect dad for me!

"Hey, did you hear the one about the duck and the papaya?"